ROSELIA and the ANCIENT WARRIORS

The Mermaids of
Crystal Cay

Roselia and the Ancient Warriors

J. B. Moonstar

Published By: The Little Horsemen an imprint of 4 Horsemen Publications, Inc.

The Little Horsemen Publications
℅ 4 Horsemen Publications, Inc.
PO Box 419
Sylva, NC 28779
4horsemenpublications.com
info@4horsemenpublications.com

Cover by J. Kotick
Typesetting by Niki Tantillo
Edited by Laura Mita

Library of Congress Control Number: 2023938109

Paperback ISBN-13: 979-8-8232-0199-5
Hardcover ISBN-13: 979-8-8232-0201-5
Audiobook ISBN-13: 979-8-8232-0198-8
Ebook ISBN-13: 979-8-8232-0200-8

Dedication

This book is dedicated to all the conservation groups working to help the horseshoe crabs recover from the continual onslaught by humans. Many groups are fighting for these wonderful undersea creatures, including Defenders of Wildlife, National Geographic, the Ocean Conservancy, and the National Wildlife Federation, among many others. Thank you for your hard work and dedication!

TABLE OF CONTENTS

Dedication v
Chapter One
    Danger Enters Protected Waters! 1
Chapter Two
    Michelle Joins the Team 6
Chapter Three
    Roselia's New Mission 10
Chapter Four
    Water for the Captives 14
Chapter Five
    Waiting to Start the Rescue 19
Chapter Six
    Help from Knocker 24
Chapter Seven
    Not to Be Seen 30
Chapter Eight
    Continuing the Escape Plan 34
Chapter Nine
    Change in Plans 38
Chapter Ten
    Slipping Away 43
Chapter Eleven
    Covering Up the Escape 47

CHAPTER TWELVE
    FIRST OBSTACLES ENCOUNTERED..............51
CHAPTER THIRTEEN
    CROSSING THE CHANNEL 56
CHAPTER FOURTEEN
    BACK TO WHERE IT BEGAN 60
CHAPTER FIFTEEN
    MERMAIDS TO THE RESCUE...................65
CHAPTER SIXTEEN
    RETURNING HOME 70

NOTE FROM AUTHOR 74
BOOK CLUB QUESTIONS.........................76
ABOUT THE AUTHOR...........................77

Chapter One

Danger Enters Protected Waters!

Roselia watched as the long procession of horseshoe crabs advanced from the deeper ocean floor toward the shallow water and sandy beaches. Every spring since she could remember, these beautiful creatures joined in a migration to the beaches near Crystal Cay. Alleana, the leader of the mermaid pod of Crystal Cay, asked Roselia to watch over this year's migration. Roselia was to discover why the numbers of horseshoe crabs had been declining over the past several years, as this decline was affecting the entire ecosystem.

Swimming a little closer, she saw the horseshoe crabs moving in silent unison, the light from the full moon filtering down through the water to guide their way. Their circular dome-shaped shells covered their entire bodies, including their legs, giving them the appearance of gliding effortlessly across the sea floor, what an exquisite sight! She knew their species had survived unchanged for millions of years, and they had been given the title of ancient warriors because of their ability to survive as a species longer than almost any other creature, even the giant ones!

Things look good tonight, Roselia thought, as many horseshoe crabs passed below her heading toward the beach. Maybe this year would be a good year for the horseshoe crabs, and so a better year for all the other creatures who depend on them to survive.

Her thoughts were interrupted as a large shadow crossed overhead, blocking the moonlight for several moments as it moved ahead of her and toward the crabs. Looking up to the surface of the water, she realized a human boat was entering the protected area, an area her friend Michelle told her was off-limits to humans. She learned about humans many years ago and of the dangers they caused to all sea creatures; they were to be avoided at all costs!

This intrusion into this underwater safe space worried Roselia. Although she had been told by Alleana to avoid humans and knew she should leave as soon as they appeared, she just couldn't leave. She had to see why this human boat was here in protected waters, and she would not leave these sea creatures alone if they needed her help! She rationalized she would still be following Alleana's directions if she watched from deeper water so she would not be seen—that was the most important rule—don't be seen!

The boat approached slowly, the rumble noises stopped, and it continued moving, drifting silently toward the shore. Roselia stayed in the deeper water as a large object dropped into the water and landed on the sea floor, anchoring the boat. Jumping off the boat and into shallow water only a few human foot-lengths deep, a human creature pulled a large tub behind it with a rope. Stopping to attach the tub's rope to its belt, the human then started peering into the water.

As she watched this behavior, she tried to figure out where it would lead, anxiously watching as the human approached the horseshoe crabs moving into the shallow water before her. She was getting worried—*this can't be good for the crabs!*

Moving quietly through the water, the human used the moonlight to locate and sneak up on the horseshoe crabs as they entered the sandy shallows. Horseshoe crabs have long thin tails they use to maneuver—and the human was grabbing them by their tails and throwing them into its giant tub!

From the deeper water, she could hear the captured crabs crying for help, not knowing what was happening to them, and Roselia tried to figure out a way to stop the human. The water where the human was walking was too shallow for her. *What can I do to stop this*? She watched in dismay; using only moonlight, this human was able to grab the horseshoe crabs before they could sense its approach, and soon the tub was full!

The human said something as it struggled to lift the full tub onto the back of the boat. While unable to understand human speak, she got the message the human was angry, and she hoped it would go away! But it didn't! It grabbed another tub and started again. She had to do something!

"You must all head to deeper water now!" she called to them softly but urgently. "Quickly! The humans are here!"

The horseshoe crabs started turning, moving, bumping into, and crawling over each other trying to find the source of the danger and head away from it. The confusion in the water played into the hands of the human, and it kept grabbing and throwing more crabs into the tub.

"Come to my voice!" Roselia urged, trying to get them to head toward her and deeper water. She did not think the human would follow if the water was deep. "This way, that's right! Come this way!" She continued calling to them as she was getting them to come back into the deeper water, away from the human.

Roselia knew horseshoe crab's eyes were small, but they had many—up to ten she had been told! There were two tiny eyes in the front to detect movement and see ultraviolet light, the others were located at various spots throughout the body also to detect movement, including one near its mouth and one near its tail. But a human hidden by darkness was an unknown danger they could not see or avoid.

"Follow my voice!" Roselia called out again, "I'm in the deeper water. It won't follow you here!"

Many of the horseshoe crabs had been able to turn back and were passing Roselia on their way to the deep; however, Roselia watched in horror as the human filled another two tubs with crabs, four tubs in all! She had to rescue them, but what could she do?

"Keep heading this way!" she called out again, getting the crabs to continue their escape. *Who can I get to help? I can't do this rescue alone!* She got an idea—it just might work! After calling to the crabs one more time, she headed out to deeper water. Hiding behind some rocks so the human would not see her, she raised her head out of the water. Looking east to the full moon as it started its journey across the sky, she called out loudly. "Guardian, please find Knocker. I need him now!"

She knew the human would not understand her mermaid speak; it would sound like what Michelle described as a human emergency siren. The human did hear something. It stopped unloading another tub from the boat and looked around, peering into the darkness, trying to see where the siren was coming from. It then turned quickly and climbed back onto its boat, pulled up the weight, started the rumbling sound, and headed away in the dark with four tubs of horseshoe crabs loaded on board!

Remembering how Knocker and Michelle helped Alleana in a previous rescue, Roselia knew there was hope for these illegally captured creatures. However, this rescue was going to need help from the air and land as well as the sea—and it needed to happen tonight! This was an emergency!

As Roselia stayed hidden by the rocks with her head above water, she heard large wings flapping in the air above, and then scratching sounds as something landed on the rocks behind her. Turning, she saw Knocker, a fantastically large dragon, his green eyes glowing and his blue-green scales shimmering in the moonlight.

In a soft whisper, he called out into the darkness. "I'm here. Who called for help?"

"Knocker, thank you so much for coming!" Roselia whispered back with relief that help had arrived. "I need your help to rescue some horseshoe crabs stolen from the protected place. We need to get Michelle too. Here is my plan!"

Chapter Two

Michelle Joins the Team

After discussing the situation and making plans with her dragon friend Knocker, Roselia headed toward Michelle's home. Michelle lived several human miles from where Roselia and Knocker thought the human and its boat would be heading, and Knocker was following the boat. She and Michelle would meet him as soon as possible at the dock.

As she swam, she thought about Michelle, the only human Alleana's pod could trust. Michelle had helped Alleana and Knocker rescue a baby manatee and had shown extreme kindness and bravery during the rescue. Since then, she and Michelle had met several times, discussing the dangerous situations created by humans involving several of Crystal Cay's inhabitants, including the horseshoe crabs. That is how Roselia knew the area where the crabs were taken was off-limits to humans—a place where all creatures, both above and below the water, were to be safe!

Getting closer to Michelle's home, she surfaced and watched carefully. She could see through the clear walls of the home and saw Michelle talking to her mother. The two humans talked for a few minutes, and then Roselia saw the older human leave the area. Knowing Michelle's mother usually worked during dark hours, she listened for the rumbling sound, which would indicate the mother had left Michelle's home for the night.

After hearing the rumbling move away from the home, Roselia got closer. Michelle moved back and forth in the house for a few minutes, and then left the front room also, going into the back portion of the house. Sitting on a flat rock, she was watching as the moon rose in the east.

Roselia called to her, "Michelle, I need your help!" Knowing Michelle would not understand her mermaid speak, she knew the call would let Michelle know one of the mermaids from Alleana's pod was out there and wanted to talk with her.

Michelle stood up and looked toward the water. Roselia swam closer. *She heard me!* Calling out once again, "Michelle, please come down to the dock!"

Reacting quickly once she heard the second call, Michelle tapped her side pocket, checking for something, and then ran down to the dock. She looked around her and sat on the dock, calling out a response. Roselia couldn't understand her but knew they had to connect, as she needed Michelle's help to save the horseshoe crabs.

Moving next to the dock, Roselia surfaced again and start talking quickly, "Michelle, I need your help to save some horseshoe crabs that have been captured in the pro-tected area!"

Shaking her head and pointing to her ears, Michelle let Roselia know she couldn't understand. Holding up her hand to motion Roselia to wait, Michelle pulled a small fish statuette out of her pocket and held it tightly in her hand as she jumped into the water. It was the magic amulet Alleana had given her after Ethan's rescue and was about three inches long and an inch and a half tall.

Once in the water, she held the small amulet in both hands and quickly said the magic words allowing her to become a mermaid. Within a few seconds, Michelle was transformed into a mermaid! Her torso and legs had become a long slender fish body and tail, and a small satchel at her side replaced her shorts pocket where she kept her magic amulet safe. Her arms were bare and free to use for swimming!

"Hi, Roselia," Michelle said, putting the small fish amulet in the satchel for safe keeping once the transformation was complete. "What is happening. Can I help you with something?"

"Greetings, Michelle!" Roselia replied quickly, "Yes, I need your help. We have an urgent situation developing, and the mermaid pod and I cannot handle it alone."

"What do you need?" Michelle asked, her voice full of concern. She had not seen Roselia this stressed before, something must be very wrong!

"This evening, I watched a human taking horseshoe crabs from a place where you learned all wildlife is protected," Roselia continued anxiously. "I was observing the area where the humans are not to enter, as Alleana asked me to watch and report on the horseshoe crab activity under the full moon. However, tonight I saw a human boat come into the protected area, and a human took many, many horseshoe crabs. They are being stored in the human's boat, and I fear the worst for them."

"What can we do?" Michelle asked. "How can we rescue them from the boat?"

"I can't get into the boat," Roselia replied, her voice stressed. "But you can, would you help me rescue these crabs?"

"If they are on the boat, how can we get to them?" Michelle asked again, trying to figure out how they could succeed on Roselia's quest.

"I have also contacted Knocker," Roselia answered. "He was going to follow the boat while I came here to get you. Between the three of us, we should be able to save them!"

"Of course, I will be glad to help!" Michelle said in a reassuring voice as she remembered her encounter with Knocker, a dragon from Ituria's Island. "What are the plans so far?"

"Well," Roselia said, "Knocker has seen this boat before, and based on recent activity Knocker observed on the beaches close to the inlet, we think the horseshoe crabs will be taken to a human-built pond near a large human building next to the river. We need to rescue them before they are taken into the building from the pond. They are in great danger! These crabs were taken from the protected area, the area to be safe for all creatures. We need to stop them before they are taken into the human building!" Roselia said nervously. She needed to rescue the horseshoe crabs, and needed to do it now!

"If they were taken from that area, we will get them back. We can do this!" Michelle exclaimed. "What is your plan?"

"First, we must get to the boat. Knocker will be waiting for us where it normally docks." Roselia replied. "The rescue must be tonight!"

Chapter Three

ROSELIA'S NEW MISSION

"Let's go then!" Michelle replied, ready to help her mermaid friend. "We will rescue them tonight! I need to be back before sunrise, though, before my mom gets home, okay?"

"I promise you will be home on time, my good friend Michelle. Thank you! It will take many of your minutes to reach where Knocker says the boat will rest, so we must go now. I will update you on the way!" Roselia said quickly, then immediately turned and dived under the surface of the water.

Michelle dived in also, following Roselia. As a mermaid, Michelle was able to see well underwater even in the darkness of night. Her eyes could see shapes and movements outlined before her, even though there was little light underwater. As she swam in Roselia's direction, she saw Roselia look back, waving for her to hurry. Michelle quickly caught up and stayed next to Roselia.

As she was swimming, Michelle thought back to when she and Roselia first met. While all mermaids had their own original coloring, each beautiful in their own way, Roselia was strikingly beautiful. Her hair was a light blonde, which was a lovely contrast to her medium lavender skin tone; her torso was a deep plum with violet and white trimming on her tail and fins. She wore a headband to keep her hair away from her face, looking almost like the front part of a human helmet, but it did not detract from her beauty. Rather, it framed her large violet eyes.

At first, Michelle thought such a colorful palate would be easily visible underwater; however, when she saw Roselia swimming one day near the kelp gardens, she was surprised at how the blue-green water blended all the colors together, and Roselia mixed in with the seagrasses quite nicely—she was almost invisible.

After Alleana introduced them, Michelle learned Roselia had been a mermaid for more than five hundred human years. Michelle was surprised, as Roselia looked only about twelve or thirteen in human years—at least her human half. Alleana explained mermaids don't age as humans do, and their human features remained the same for most of their life, no matter how old they were. There have been reports of mermaids in other pods living up to a thousand years!

Swimming closer to Roselia, Michelle asked, "What have you learned about this human building from the crabs? Why are they taken in there?"

"I have talked to some of the horseshoe crabs I have seen released from this building. The stories they tell me are unbelievable!" Roselia said, still swimming swiftly under the water. "As we've discussed, Alleana asked me to watch the crabs as they come to the shallows this spring. We are trying to figure out why their numbers are going down. I suspect this human building has something to do with it," she added as anger crept into her voice.

"Right," Michelle agreed. "We were able to locate the protected area near here. Is that where they were taken from?"

"Yes!" Roselia replied, the terror of the scene she witnessed still with her. "I was watching those who were supposed to be safe, but they were not! A human boat came through, and the human filled four large tubs with the crabs. I saw how they were grabbed by their tails and thrown into the tub. It was awful! They were crying out for help. It must have hurt!

"One of the crabs I talked to earlier this week, Carlos, said he had been taken to a dirty shallow pond and left there without food for days. Then he was taken into the building where they pierced his skin and drained his blood until he was very weak, then he was thrown back into the bay." Roselia paused as the memory of her conversation with Carlos brought renewed sadness. "Carlos said he was very tired after his ordeal, but no help was forthcoming from the humans. After being starved and his blood drained, the humans took him and the other crabs and just dumped them back in the water. He was barely able to make it back to the deep water."

"I have been reading on this since our last discussion," Michelle said as they swam toward the inlet, "and it seems the humans in a local medical laboratory drain about 30 percent of horseshoe crab blood for medicines. They claim that it doesn't hurt the crabs and they return them to the water unharmed. Yet recent reports indicate up to thirty percent of the horseshoe crabs die once they are released."

"I know!" Roselia exclaimed. "Carlos said his friend, Hector, did not make it back home—he does not know what happened to him."

"Roselia, how many humans were involved in capturing the horseshoe crabs tonight?" Michelle asked, wondering how many they might be up against.

"There was only one," Roselia replied. "It looked like it was struggling when it was moving the full tubs—maybe it will work to our advantage."

Roselia slowed down and motioned for Michelle to stop beside her. Roselia pointed to the surface and a boat moving above them. "We are almost there," she said. "This boat must be heading for the same dock Knocker identified to me as where the human docks its boat. Let's go around it and see if Knocker is already at the dock, okay?"

"Okay, I'll follow you!" Michelle called out as Roselia turned to go around the boat toward the human docks.

"You must stay underwater, though, Michelle!" Roselia warned. "Remember there are lights near the dock, so you can be seen if you surface. We will surface under the dock only if we won't be seen. Just follow my lead!"

"Will do!" Michelle replied, following Roselia around the hull of the boat and to the dock beyond.

Chapter Four

WATER FOR THE CAPTIVES

Staying just below the surface, Roselia searched the dock trying to see if Knocker had arrived. "Yes, he's there!" she whispered to Michelle and headed in a little closer. "Let's wait for the boat to dock. We don't want to get caught in the ropes or its propellers. Once it is tied up, we will get underneath the dock and surface so Knocker will know we are there."

Staying underwater, Roselia and Michelle watched as the hull of the boat moved next to the dock and pulled alongside, stopping its movement. Roselia motioned for Michelle to follow her as they swam under the dock, popping their heads up underneath the section where Knocker was standing.

Knocker's appearance had drastically changed since Roselia saw him last. Roselia knew Knocker had a magic potion allowing him to transform into a human shape to blend in with humans when he needed to do so. He now had the appearance of a tall boy about thirteen or fourteen years old with shoulder-length black hair, wearing a t-shirt and jeans, with a satchel hanging over his shoulder. She knew he kept a magical translation stone in the satchel, which allowed him to communicate with humans. He would need it to talk with Michelle if she transformed back into a human to help the trapped horseshoe crabs.

Knocker was talking to a human on the dock; however, she could not hear the conversation as they were discussing something quietly. She saw Knocker pause and look quickly about, and then he continued with the conversation. After a few more minutes, the human left and started walking down the dock, heading toward land.

Knocker stood still for a few moments to take a few deep breaths in the night air, and then called out softly, "Roselia, are you here?"

Roselia swam out from under the dock to where Knocker could see her and whispered. "Yes, Knocker, I'm here. What have you found out?"

"I have identified the human who stole the crabs and his boat, and I was just talking with him." Pausing for just a moment as he took another breath, he continued. "Is Michelle here too? I can smell her presence."

"Hi, Knocker, I'm here." Michelle said as she swam next to Roselia. "Nice to see you again! Sorry it is under such circumstances; however, I'm glad you came to help Roselia!"

"Hi, Michelle, I am always glad to help my friends. I have learned a lot in the last few minutes." Knocker whispered. "I have convinced the human to get some food, but we will have to be quick as he will only be gone for a short time. Roselia, you are correct, his hull is full of horseshoe crabs, and he plans on delivering them tonight under cover of darkness. I suggested I wanted to make some money and could help him move his catch for payment, and he said he would think about it over his meal."

Turning to Michelle, Knocker continued. "Michelle, the first step Roselia and I discussed was to get some water to the crabs in the buckets. These creatures can survive out of water as long as they are provided with enough water so that their gills don't dry out. We need to supply them with some water now to keep them alive. I have also learned the horseshoe crabs are being stored in the lower level of the boat." Knocker turned and pointed to a round portal on the side of the boat.

"Michelle, you will need to transform back into a human and climb through the portal over there. It leads directly to the crabs," Knocker said as he pointed to the portal large enough for Michelle to slip through, but not Knocker, even in his human form. "You should find the crabs in the bottom level of the ship near the front. I will tell them who you are and that you are there to pour water into the tubs so they will not be frightened by your presence."

"I can do that!" Michelle agreed. "How can I get up to the dock once I transform? Is there a ladder I can use?"

"Yes, there is a ladder over there," Knocker said, pointing to a ladder leading from the water. "You can use that one. Here are four jugs you can fill up. They will fit through the porthole." Knocker carefully dropped four empty half-gallon jugs in the water next to Michelle. She gathered them by their handles and submerged them to fill them with water.

"Roselia, we need to make sure Michelle is out of the boat before the human gets back," Knocker said.

"I agree. I will find a position where I can see the entrance to the dock and will come back once I see the human returning," Roselia replied then asked about the captives. "Knocker, did you find out how many crabs were taken?"

"The human said he has four large tubs of crabs on the boat," Knocker answered. "He estimated about 40 crabs in each tub so that would be about 160 crabs confined below."

"We need to save them!" Roselia said anxiously as she turned and headed to her watchpoint. "I'll let you know as soon as I see him coming back. I'm on my way!"

"Michelle," Knocker said as Roselia disappeared under the water, "please join me when you have transformed so we can start."

"I'll be there in just a moment!" Michelle said as she turned and swam toward the ladder, using her mermaid tail to propel her as she held the four jugs full of water.

Once Michelle reached the ladder, she balanced the water jugs on the ladder steps. Reaching into her satchel, she took out her magic fish amulet. Holding it tightly, she whispered, "I am human, I am human, I am human!"

The magic amulet transformed her back into a human in just a few moments, and she made sure to put the amulet into her shorts pocket before doing anything else because she didn't want to lose the amulet! After climbing up the ladder, she picked up the water jugs and quickly walked over to the portal Knocker pointed out earlier. It was close enough to the dock for her to reach, and she was able to pull it open and turned to wait for Knocker, who had walked over to hold the water jugs while she climbed into the portal.

Moving closer to the portal, Knocker called softly into the opening. "Listen to me all inside. We are sending in a human to bring you water so you can survive in the tubs. We will be attempting to rescue you soon. Please be ready when we give the word!"

Michelle heard horseshoe crabs bumping into and climbing over each other as they clamored around the large tubs in the hull where they were trapped. They were ready to be rescued!

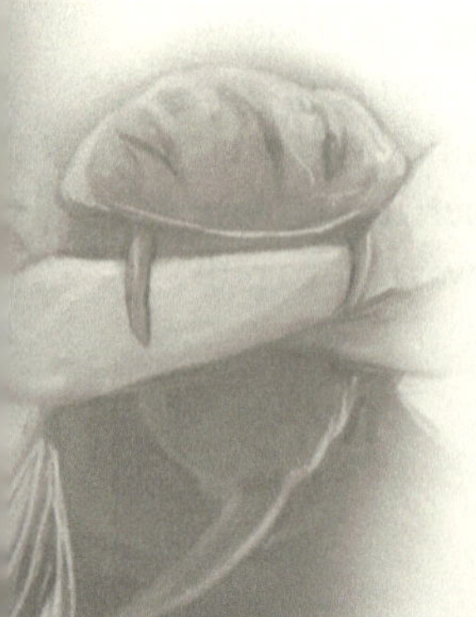

Chapter Five

Waiting to Start the Rescue

"Okay, now, Michelle!" Knocker said softly. "And make sure the water is spread around evenly, as they will all need to have access to the water to keep their gills moistened."

Nodding as Knocker handed her the first jug of water, Michelle replied, "Okay, I'll make sure!" She climbed through the open portal and stepped on a bench underneath, looking around the hull of the boat. There was a light hung near the middle giving some light into the bottom hull. Looking around quickly, she saw four large tubs full of horseshoe crabs; the crabs were piled one on top of the other, crammed into the tubs until there was no room left.

"Hurry, Michelle!" Knocker urged. "You have to be quick!"

As Michelle poured the first jug into the first tub, she made sure to pour a little on each crab on the top, also pouring in any spaces between the crabs so all the layers would get water. As she did, she called out to them. "Hang in there. Help is on the way!" She knew they wouldn't understand her, but she hoped the tone of her voice would relay she was there to help. Handing the empty jug through the portal and back to Knocker, he passed through another for her to take. Within a few minutes, all four jugs of water had been poured into the tubs, allowing the crabs to survive for a little longer without being submerged in water.

"Okay, Knocker, here is the last one, all emptied!" Michelle called to him as she passed the last jug back to him. Now it was her turn to get back out onto the dock. "I am getting ready to make my way back through the portal!"

Knocker put the empty jugs into a storage box on the dock so they would not fall into the water, then headed back to the boat to help Michelle.

Roselia had been watching carefully for the human to come back into the dock area. There he was, just stepping onto the dock! Swiftly swimming back to Knocker, she surfaced and warned, "He is on his way back! Get Michelle out of the boat now and back in the water—quickly!"

"Michelle!" whispered Knocker into the portal, "You must leave now—here take my hand! We must get you out of there!"

Michelle's hand appeared through the portal and Knocker helped her out onto the dock. "Michelle," Knocker whispered urgently, "Roselia says he is on his way back, you must get off the dock now!"

Nodding, Michelle ran over to the ladder and climbed quickly back into the water. Holding her amulet tight, she whispered, "I am a mermaid, I am a mermaid, I am a mermaid!" As soon as the transformation was complete, she put away the amulet, submerged beneath the surface, and swam over to Roselia who was back under the dock and out of sight.

They were all listening to the footsteps of the human approaching the boat when Michelle realized the portal hatch was still open!

Michelle quickly swam closer to Knocker and softly called to him from under the dock, "Knocker, close the portal!"

Knocker nodded and stepped over to the boat, reached over, and quickly closed the portal. He stood in front of it to block the view of the portal so the human could not see what he was doing. After it was closed, he pretended to be looking at some ropes hanging on the side of the boat as the human walked up to him.

"These are nice knots tied on the ropes. I guess I'll have to learn to tie them if I'm to work on a boat," Knocker said as he pointed to the knots.

"Yep, boy," the human answered, "there's a lot to learn if you are going to make your living off the sea. A lot to learn! If you still want to join me, I will pay you for your time. I checked with my contacts, and I am clear for a delivery tonight."

"Where would you take them at night?" Knocker asked. "Wouldn't it be easier to deliver your catch during the day?"

"Well, these particular horseshoe crabs are destined for a special place." He responded evasively. "The lab where they will be delivered doesn't mind where I get the crabs, as long as I don't get caught."

"What do you mean?" Knocker looked at him quizzically and asked, "Why should you worry about getting caught?"

"No reason, no reason at all!" the human said, getting defensive. "I just need to make my quota, and I get paid. These crabs will net me a good pay, and I'll share a bit with you for your help unloading them. Sound good?"

"Okay," Knocker replied. "As long as I'm not going to be getting into any trouble by helping you. I may need the money, but I don't want to break the law."

"You will be fine. You can depend on old Joe here to keep you safe, okay, buddy?" Joe answered, trying to reassure him. "By the way, what's your name, young man?"

"My name is Marcus," Knocker replied. "Well, let's get on with it then!"

"Okay," Joe replied. "The first thing you'll need to do is to hold the rope hooked onto the edge there, and when I get the engine started and warmed up, you will push the boat away from the dock and jump on. Can you do that?"

"I think so," Knocker answered. "Haven't done it before, but there's always a first time."

As Joe went over and started the engine, Knocker looked back at the area where Michelle and Roselia were submerged.

Roselia surfaced near Knocker and whispered, "Michelle and I will follow the boat. See you there!"

Knocker nodded and looked quickly back to Joe, holding the rope tightly to keep the boat next to the dock. After running the engines for a few minutes, Joe signaled for Knocker to push the boat out and jump on. Knocker gave the edge of the boat a hard push and then jumped quickly onto the back deck.

"Good job, boy," Joe exclaimed. "I'll make a seaman out of you yet!"

"We shall see how the trip goes," Knocker replied. "By the way, where are we heading?"

"Nothing for you to worry about. No need to know where we are going." Joe answered guardedly, glancing over at Knocker. "Just know if we get everything unloaded, I'll pay you a fair wage for your work, okay?"

Knocker nodded then looked over the back of the boat, and he could see two v-shaped wakes—Roselia and Michelle were following right behind the boat! Now for step two!

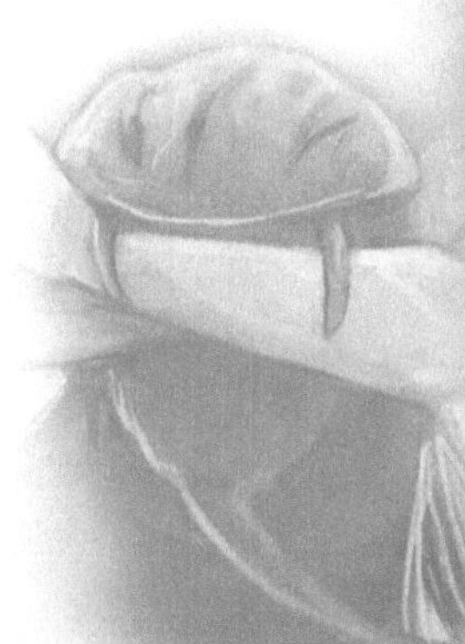

Chapter Six

HELP FROM KNOCKER

Michelle and Roselia swam behind the boat, making sure to stay clear of the propeller and its wake. Occasionally, they would see Knocker glance back, looking for them to confirm they were keeping up with the boat—Joe was going very fast in the dark without any running lights. It was a full moon tonight, so there was a soft light reflecting on the water and the land beyond.

Turning away from the bay, the boat headed upriver and traveled several more minutes before heading toward the shore. As it maneuvered toward a small dock outside of a large building, Roselia waved to Michelle, motioning to follow her. Heading closer to the shore, Roselia picked up the end of a large piece of plastic tarp to show to Michelle.

"Look, Michelle, Knocker found this tarp, and he said it looked like something we could use," Roselia said as she held up the edge of a large plastic sheet, about twelve-foot square. "My plan with Knocker is to wait until all the crabs have been unloaded into the human-built pond and let the human leave in his boat. We could then take the tarp and slip it under them. That's where you come in."

"I don't follow," Michelle said. "How are we going to get the tarp underneath them?"

Roselia swam over to where the concrete seawall created one side of the human pond.

"I will stay here in the river on the side of the pond close to the water and reach over the side. See how the edge is right against the seawall here?"

Michelle nodded as she looked at the concrete borders of the pond, one side touching the water, the wall itself was only about a foot over the height of the water in the river. She checked the depth of the water and confirmed it was deep enough for Roselia's plan, with the water being about five feet deep on the waterside of the seawall. As she was looking at the seawall, she saw what looked like a sliding door on the side of the wall that could be opened to let the water in or out as needed.

Roselia continued explaining her plans. "If you look at the human pond, it is about 12 of your foot measurements wide, and about 30 of your foot measurements long. There are rock walls, and the water looks about three to four feet deep." Moving closer to the seawall and reaching her hands out of the water and touching the top of the seawall, Roselia continued. "You can become a human and get on the other side of the pond, and together, we will move the tarp along the bottom, slipping it under the crabs and allowing them to crawl on top as we slowly pull it along the bottom and get it centered in the pond. The crabs on the far side can get on once we have it positioned."

"Okay, I can see how this would work," Michelle replied, running the process through her mind. "But how will this help the crabs?"

"Once all the crabs are contained on top of the tarp, Knocker will return and pick it up with the crabs, carrying them away and back to their home in the refuge. It will be dark, so he can fly in!" Roselia answered. "That way we can keep the crabs all together until they are safe."

"What a great plan!" Michelle said enthusiastically. "We will need to make sure we tell the crabs what we are doing—you will have to tell them if I am human. They won't understand me."

"I can let them know while we are moving the tarp through the pond," Roselia replied. "You are right, the horseshoe crabs need to know why we are doing it, or they may fight the tarp or run away."

Observing from near the seawall, Roselia and Michelle saw the poacher's boat pull alongside the small dock just outside the retention pond. Once it was tied up, they watched Joe and Knocker bring out the first tub of crabs. It was about five feet in diameter and very heavy to carry; Joe was straining to keep his side of the tub from dropping. Michelle listened closely, knowing that Roselia would not understand the conversation.

"Hey, kid," Joe said as he struggled to carry one side of the tub, "just set it here in the dark next to the pond, okay?" They put the tub down in a section near the dock that was not lit so that they would be hidden by darkness.

Looking around the pond, Michelle saw there were a few small ground-level lights located on the walkway from the dock to the retention pond with larger streetlights in the parking lot and next to the building beyond them. One tall light was on the far corner of the retention pond, but it didn't light the entire pond, and Joe was using the darkness to hide their presence.

"This is what we're going to do, Marcus," Joe said as they placed the tub down next to the closest wall of the retention pond. "Let's stay in the shadows over here. We need to get all four tubs of crabs in the retention pond, so we need to throw them in to spread them out as much as possible. We can't just dump them all in one place; they won't fit."

"Well, what if we move the tubs around to different areas, then we could dump them in, and it would be safer for them," Knocker countered. "Throwing them sounds like they may get hurt when they hit the water."

"No, that will take too long!" Joe exclaimed anxiously. "I just need to get these into the pond and leave before anyone sees us here."

Picking up a crab by the tail, Joe flung it far into the pond.

Roselia and Michelle gasped as they saw the crab thrown, hearing its cry for help as it flew through the air, crashing hard into the water.

Roselia turned to Michelle, her eyes wide, "We have to do something, Michelle. Should I call the other mermaids?"

Michelle quickly put her arm around Roselia's shoulders to comfort her and whispered, "Don't call out, Roselia. Let's give Knocker a chance to do something! If he can't, I'll do something to stop him! We won't let this continue!"

Michelle saw Knocker glance toward them when he

heard her whispering to Roselia. Knocker knew she was doing her best to keep Roselia calm so that they could go forward with the plan. However, there had to be a way to stop this needless harming of the crabs. She watched as Knocker put his hand over the tub to stop any more from being thrown, and he looked at Joe, trying to control his anger.

"Throwing them by their tail has got to hurt them," Knocker said. "Can't you be more careful? Surely, the people you are delivering these for would want them in good condition, right?"

"Well, boy," Joe said, "I've been told it don't matter what shape they are in. Just get them delivered, and I'll get paid. Besides, a lot of them will die anyway. As long as I get paid by how many I deliver, it don't matter if they are alive, hurt, or even dead when they get here."

Joe pushed Knocker's hand out of the way and picked up another crab.

Roselia watched, knowing Knocker was trying to control his fury at this cruel attitude; he had to remain calm until all the crabs were put into the water and the poacher left. She couldn't understand Joe's side of the conversation, but she could understand Knocker and he was doing all he could to protect the crabs.

"Okay," Knocker said, "Let's try and get them in so they won't get hurt. Look, I'll move the tubs around, okay? You put these crabs here—nice and easy—and I'll get the other tubs and put them in around the pond, so it will be easier for them to get into the water."

"Boy, those tubs are heavy!" Joe called out to him. "After trying to lift one of them, you'll be slinging them into the water, just like me!" Joe looked at the crab in his hand, but he didn't throw it this time; he set it down at the edge of the water and gave it a push—it slid into the water. "Let's wait to see if you can do better!" he grumbled.

Knocker didn't respond but went onto the boat to get the second tub. He got off the boat holding the second tub level and walked it carefully to the side of the pond away from Joe. Gently pouring in the crabs so they didn't crash into each other or the water, he emptied the tub as he softly called to the crabs. "You need to be ready when the mermaids show up, they will have a tarp for you to crawl into, and we will rescue you."

When he got back to the boat for the third tub, Joe stopped dropping crabs in the water and walked over to him.

"How did you do that?" Joe asked in disbelief. "Those tubs have to weigh at least a hundred pounds each!"

"It's okay. I work out at school; I'm on the weight-lifting team." Knocker replied calmly. "This is easy for me, and the crabs don't get hurt in the process." Continuing onto the boat to get the third tub, he took it to the other side of the pond and dumped it slowly, conveying the same message, and allowing the crabs to get into the water without being hurt.

"I may hire you full-time, boy!" Joe said as he watched Knocker walk off the boat with the fourth tub. "I could use your help on my fishing expeditions, for sure!"

Chapter Seven

NOT TO BE SEEN

"Let's see how this job goes, and then maybe we will talk," Knocker replied without emotion; he was focusing on remaining calm and getting the horseshoe crabs into the water so that Roselia and Michelle could start step two of the rescue. After getting the fourth tub of crabs into the water he whispered, "Spread the word! As soon as the boat leaves, be prepared to be rescued!"

After he took the fourth tub back to the boat, he started helping Joe with the crabs in the first bucket. "See, no one gets hurt, and you get all the crabs into the pond."

"What does it matter to you if the crabs get hurt?" Joe asked suspiciously, starting to wonder if he should have brought this kid on his delivery.

"It matters a lot to me. Every creature has the right to be treated with respect," Knocker answered calmly, looking Joe in the eyes.

"Well, these guys are just going to be drained and then thrown out to sea, so being nice ain't going to matter much!" Joe argued, his voice getting louder as his suspicions grew.

"It matters to them!" Knocker said defiantly, his anger creeping into his voice. "Cruelty to animals is not tolerated where I live."

"Well, I guess you'll just have to ..." Joe started sarcastically but stopped talking as they both turned to look at a flashlight beam heading their way from the direction of the building.

A voice yelled out, "Hey, you! What are you doing out there?" The holder of the flashlight was quickly moving their way, keeping the flashlight beam on them.

Michelle swam along the seawall so that she could get closer to Joe and Knocker; she needed to hear what was going on. This new human may complicate their plan to rescue the horseshoe crabs! Roselia followed close behind because, although she couldn't understand human speak, she knew another human might complicate their rescue plans, and they needed to be prepared.

"Okay, Marcus, this is the story," Joe whispered quietly as his tone changed to overly friendly, wanting Knocker to play along. "We were just fishing here, nothing for the guard to see, okay?"

"Why?" Knocker asked in a normal tone. "Aren't we supposed to be here?"

"Well, yes, of course, we are supposed to be here!" Joe said, but he was getting a little nervous. "Just play along with whatever I say, okay?"

"It may depend on what you say," Knocker answered decisively. "I will not lie for you; be aware of this now before you try and cast a story to cover your presence here."

"What do you mean? You said you were going to help me, so you will do what I tell you or you won't get paid.

Got it!" Joe argued back, now trying to bully Knocker into doing what he said.

"I will not lie for you," Knocker repeated quietly as they both turned to see who was approaching from the building area.

Walking up to them was a security guard, and she was shining her flashlight on both Joe and Knocker. Since Joe and Knocker were standing in a darker section, the guard could only see two figures in the dark.

"Okay boys, this is private property," the guard started as she got closer. Looking at Joe and Knocker carefully, she continued. "What are you doing here?"

"We were just fishing off the dock. Didn't know it was private property," Joe said, trying to sound apologetic. "We thought it would be a good place to fish."

"Then why aren't you on the dock fishing?" the guard replied suspiciously. "I'm going to have to get your names and report you to the guard station, okay? If you just made a mistake, it's no problem."

"No, you can't do that!" Joe replied in a hushed but stressed voice. "No one is to know I'm here, okay? Don't tell your guard station." Joe continued, trying to explain away his presence. "The lab knows I'm here delivering their crabs; these ones came from special areas. Your boss and I, we got it worked out. I deliver these at night, and he comes by in the morning and counts them. Then he pays me for how many I deliver."

"Well, it does explain why you are sneaking around here at night," the security guard said, shaking her head. "Look, you need to leave now, before anyone else sees you. If you're here when I make my next rounds, you'll be accompanying me to the guard station, got it?"

"Yes, we are on our way now!" Joe said hurriedly. "You won't be seeing us here again tonight."

Knocker looked over to where he knew Roselia and Michelle were watching and waiting for them to leave. He gave a very slight nod and then turned to head back to the boat.

"You heard the guard, Joe," Knocker said. "We need to leave now!"

"Well, we did get the horseshoe crabs in the pond, so I agree," Joe replied in a lower tone. "But I'm not sure if you're going to get a job on my boat if you don't obey my orders."

"I don't think I want to work for someone who treats living creatures so shamefully, so we are both of the same mind, aren't we?" Knocker said calmly, just wanting to get Joe to leave so the mermaids to move in.

"Well, maybe I should just leave you here then," Joe said sarcastically. "Let you find your own way home—or you can go sleep with your buddy crabs there!"

"Well, I guess in that situation, I would go to the guard station and reveal you are unloading illegally caught horseshoe crabs and passing them off as legal." Knocker countered.

"Alright, let's go!" Joe grumbled as he stomped up the dock and onto the boat and started the engines.

Michelle and Roselia watched as the boat headed back to the main docks; Knocker was standing on the back of the boat looking toward the dock and retention pond. As the boat disappeared into the darkness, Roselia motioned for Michelle to follow her.

"Knocker has done his part; now it's our turn!" she called out to Michelle as she headed to pick up the tarp and start the rescue.

Chapter Eight

Continuing the Escape Plan

Roselia took one side of the tarp, and Michelle took the other, and they pulled it along the surface of the water until they got to the seawall.

"This is where you come in, Michelle!" Roselia whispered. "You will need to turn into a human and then pull your part of the tarp over the seawall edge."

"Okay, before I do, though, call out to the horseshoe crabs and tell them I'm coming, so they are not scared of me," Michelle answered.

Roselia nodded and called out softly to the crabs. "To my friend horseshoe crabs, we are here to rescue you. My friend Michelle will turn into a human and will be pulling one side of a large piece of material into your pond. Please do not fear her human form—she is a friend. I have the other side of the tarp, and we need you to get onto the top of the material so we can lift you out of the retention pond and get you back home!"

Michelle could hear the crabs talking amongst themselves and responding to Roselia, wondering what was going on. She called to them, trying to explain. "I need to transform into a human to rescue you. Please know I mean no harm; however, in my human form, I will not understand your words. Please listen to Roselia, as she is the mermaid in charge of this rescue, and I am helping her and following her directions!"

"So, you are a mermaid who can change into a human?" came the question from one of the crabs, talking louder than the others, after he heard Michelle's message.

"Yes, I will be using mermaid magic to turn into a human to help in this rescue; however, I can't understand you when I'm a human, so you have to listen to Roselia, okay?" Michelle replied. "Please spread the word to the other crabs!"

"If you are a mermaid, then I will accept you even if you have the form of a human. I'll let the others know. Thank you for helping us!" the crab called back. Michelle could hear him calling to the other crabs, letting them know her being a human was part of the plan to rescue them.

"Roselia," Michelle said, "I will first submerge the front part of the tarp, and then we can pull it slowly. Please try and keep it in a straight line from your side, you should be able to see it moving forward as you hold onto the right side of the tarp. Once I get it positioned correctly, I'll come over and wave at you from the seawall."

"Sounds good, Michelle," Roselia answered. "I will move it to keep it straight with your side. Let's do this!"

Michelle nodded and took the small fish amulet out of her satchel and whispered, "I am human, I am human, I am human!" Within a few seconds, she was human again and hanging onto the side of the seawall. She pulled herself onto the concrete seawall and then kneeled to reach for the tarp Roselia was holding for her so that she could spread it out and they could start working it onto the bottom the retention pond.

Taking her side of the tarp, Michelle laid it flat on the south side of the pond edge, then she pulled it back so it was laying out like a large sheet of paper. As it was laid out, it was the width of the retention pond and about 12 feet back, so all the crabs would need to get onto it after it was submerged.

Roselia still had hold of the top right corner, so once the tarp was in place, Michelle looked over the seawall at Roselia and nodded, signaling she would start pushing the tarp under the water, and hopefully the crabs would be able to crawl onto the top.

Roselia called out to the crabs. "Okay, everyone, here we go! Please get onto the top of the material as it gets to you—don't run and don't fight the human holding it, please hurry!"

As Michelle got into the pond, she noticed it was not clean water, but rather it was stagnant and dirty. This couldn't be good for the crabs! The sooner they got out of here the better!

Reaching her hand down to the bottom first to make sure there were no crabs underneath it, Michelle walked on the tarp to push it to the bottom of the pond. After she got the first section of the tarp submerged, if she and Roselia pulled it carefully, it should stay submerged and give the crabs a chance to climb on top of it.

Moving the tarp slowly down so it lay flat on the bottom of the retention pond, Michelle watched as the crabs started crawling onto it behind her as she pulled it forward. The full moon was giving enough light for them to move forward with their plan. The moonlight also provided her with just enough light to allow her to look carefully before stepping on the bottom, avoiding the other crabs still on the floor of the pond.

Once it was fully submerged, she worked with Roselia to pull it along the bottom and get it centered in the pond. The water inside the pond was about three feet deep and up to her waist. As she walked, Michelle slipped on some slime on the bottom of the pond and splashed loudly in the water as she caught herself on the concrete seawall. *That was close!*

Glad she hadn't fallen into the dirty water, Michelle started walking forward again, keeping the tarp on the bottom as she and Roselia centered it to get all the crabs on top.

The clicking sound of boots on concrete and a flash of light made her turn around; she saw the guard with the flashlight heading back toward the pond! *She can't find me here! What can I do?* There was only one thing she could think of to do—Michelle reached into her pocket and held onto the small fish amulet and whispered, "I am a mermaid, I am a mermaid, I am a mermaid!"

As she transformed into a mermaid, she submerged under the dirty water. Once the transformation was complete, she stayed as still as possible—she could not be found here, either as a human or a mermaid!

Chapter Nine

Change in Plans

Looking up through the murky water, Michelle could see a light flashing over the pond. She remained as still as possible, not moving a flipper, waiting for the guard to go away again. She could feel the crabs moving around on the tarp. They wouldn't realize the lights meant someone was looking their way—but they were not the worry. She was the largest thing in this small retention pond, barely covered in three feet of dirty water. The guard wouldn't be looking for the horseshoe crabs; she knew they were there. She was trying to find what made the splash in the pond.

When Roselia saw Michelle turn into a mermaid and dive under the water, she stopped pulling on the tarp and hid behind the seawall. In the darkness, the tarp looked very similar in color to the concrete seawall facing the river, so would not draw attention to it. All they could do was wait until the guard left.

After a few minutes, the light flashes faded, and Michelle hoped she had gone away. Carefully raising her head above the waterline, Michelle looked around to see where the guard had gone. *There she is!* Seeing the guard back next to the large building, Michelle knew she had to complete the mission. Only as a human could she get the tarp positioned so it could be lifted by Knocker when he arrived. She had to change back!

Reaching into her satchel to grasp the fish amulet, she whispered, "I am human, I am human, I am human!" As soon as she transformed back, she slowly stood up, hoping her movements would not draw any further attention to their rescue mission.

"Roselia," Michelle whispered. She knew Roselia wouldn't understand human speak, but she hoped it would tell Roselia it was safe. A few moments later Roselia appeared on the other side of the seawall and nodded. They would continue!

After several more steps pulling the tarp with Roselia, Michelle saw they had gotten it positioned in the middle of the retention pond. This way, Knocker could pick up the crabs by lifting the four corners of the tarp, to carry the horseshoe crabs back to the ocean.

Staying as low as possible without putting her face in the dirty water, she slowly and carefully crossed over on the tarp. Before each step, she made sure she would not be stepping onto one of the many crabs below her. Reaching the other side of the pond, she peered over the seawall and waved to Roselia. They had gotten the tarp ready, now they just had to wait for Knocker! Michelle would wait on this side, inside the retention pond as a human, to help Knocker in his dragon form to gather up the corners of the tarp.

They didn't have to wait long! The sound of flapping wings caught Michelle's attention. She looked into the sky—could it be Knocker, or possibly it was just a large owl? It was too far away to tell at this point. However, as it got louder, she was sure it was Knocker. The flapping was slow and rhythmic with no great exertion, just a calm swishing as it got closer and closer. Once it stopped, she looked over at the dark area near the pond where Joe had hidden from the lights, wondering if Knocker would show up in the darkness next to the pond.

But he wasn't there! She heard a low growl coming from over the side of the seawall where Roselia was waiting. Michelle quickly looked over the seawall and into the river. *What is going on?* She saw Knocker in human form holding onto the seawall, and Roselia a little further out, with her head and shoulders showing above the water. *Why isn't Knocker going to rescue the crabs?*

Michelle moved closer to Roselia and Knocker. Still in human form, she asked, "What is going on? Are you going to be able to rescue the crabs?" She remembered the translation stone Knocker always carried, and now that she was within ten feet of Knocker, it would allow her to understand his dragon speak. If Roselia were close enough, Michelle would be able to understand her also, even if she remained in human form.

"Not now, Michelle, there has been a change in plans," Knocker said softly but quickly. "Listen carefully, the human is coming back. He will be here in just a few moments. You need to take this translation stone. It will allow you to talk to Roselia and the crabs in your human form."

Michelle had remembered correctly! "Yes," Michelle responded. "I remember, it works if I am within ten feet of the non-human I want to talk to, like you, Roselia, or the crabs. What shall we do now?"

"We need to make another plan!" Knocker said. "Roselia, do you have any alternatives for getting these crabs out of the pond?"

Shaking her head slowly in response, Roselia did not have another way to get them out. Her plan was to rescue them by lifting them on the tarp, and now that plan wouldn't work, they would be seen!

Thinking to herself for a moment, Michelle replied. "Listen, I saw a metal door in the pond wall on the other end. If we can get the door open, maybe we can lead them out through the door!"

Turning in the water and holding onto the seawall from the inside, she moved until she reached the metal door. "Look!" Michelle exclaimed. "If we can figure out how to break the lock, we can open this door. The other alternative I can think of is for me to hand them over the seawall one by one, and we may not have time for that."

Knocker held onto the seawall from the outside as he quickly moved over to her and the door, looking at it carefully. "So, if we open this door, the crabs will be able to get out?"

"Yes!" Michelle replied. "You can see the door goes about two feet below the waterline; this must be used to

put more water into the pond, or possibly let some out if there were too much."

Roselia swam over to the door and looked at the metal lock holding it closed. Taking the lock into her hands, Roselia looked at Knocker. "We need to break this lock, Knocker. Do you have any thoughts?"

Knocker nodded as he moved over to get a closer look at the lock in Roselia's hand. "Let me take a look at it."

Taking the lock in his hand, Knocker slowly closed his fingers around it; crushing it into several pieces, the retaining loops fell off and slipped from the latches on the door. There was no more lock to keep the door closed! "Okay, let's go with plan two!"

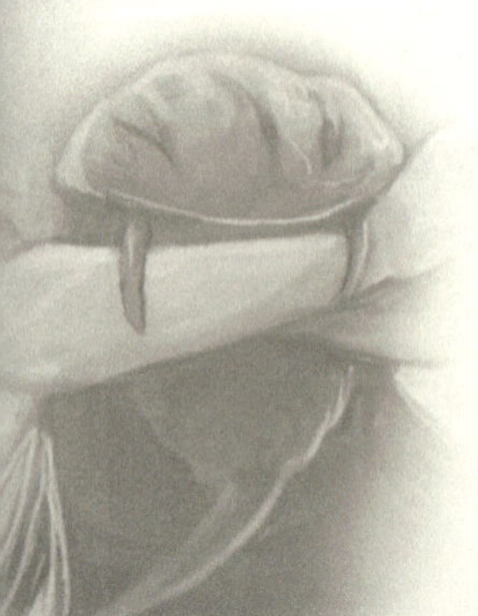

Chapter Ten

SLIPPING AWAY

Michelle opened the door from inside the retention pond, sliding it open as far as it would go. She looked at the tarp; it could not be used now to lift the crabs out of the pond. It would be too dangerous with Joe returning—but wait, maybe it would still be useful!

"Roselia," Michelle whispered, "let's make the tarp a slide, where the crabs can slip out of the pond and into the river, okay?"

"I'm not quite sure what you are talking about," Roselia replied, looking at Michelle. "What is a slide?"

"I think I see where you are going, Michelle," Knocker noted. "Let me distract Joe for a few minutes while you see if you can make an escape slide for the crabs!"

"Roselia," Michelle called softly. "I am going to open the door here and feed part of the tarp out, putting the edges of the tarp up the sides of the open door. The water level is the same inside and outside. If you hold the tarp here and I lift the far side of the tarp, we may be able to slide the crabs into the water—at least they will no longer be in the dirty pond!"

Watching Michelle spread the edges of the tarp over the door opening, Roselia understood. It would be a smooth descent, and no one would get hurt—it would be the fastest way to get them out!

"Listen, everyone," Roselia called softly to the crabs, "stay on the tarp and as close to the middle as you can get. Pass the word. The human will lift the other side so you all can slide into the water with me. Once in the water, find me and we will journey home together."

"Roselia," Michelle said, "you will need to keep the tarp tight and against the door opening, so the slide will remain steady. I am moving over to the other side now!"

Roselia pulled on the tarp, resting it on the bottom and sides of the door to make it a smooth exit for the crabs. She used her tail to hold it down tight. This way, the crabs would slide out smoothly. "Come this way everyone," she whispered to them through the open door. "Hurry!"

As Michelle started lifting the other side of the tarp, Roselia could see the crabs start to slide down and out the door. Since they were underwater, they slid under the water and were able to float down to the bottom about three feet away.

"Once you get to the bottom," Roselia called to them, "move away as fast as you can, get behind me! We need to get everyone out and then we will get you all back home!"

"Thank you!" one of the crabs replied as he slid out the door. "We heard you from inside and are all moving this way!"

Roselia could hear Michelle talking to the crabs but was too far away for the translation stone to allow her to under-stand. However, Michelle's plan was working! She watched as the tarp lifted a little at a time. As the crabs slid down into the river, the tarp would get lighter, and Michelle would be able to lift it higher.

The horseshoe crabs were sliding out quickly now, and Roselia called to them again. "Make sure you move away from the landing spot as soon as you can. There will be many more following you—get behind me. Great job everyone!"

She knew Michelle would have to lift the tarp above the waterline of the pond at some point to let all the crabs escape, and she hoped Knocker was able to distract Joe so he would not see his prize escaping.

Roselia lifted her head above water and could see Joe's boat was now at the dock; she could also hear Joe yelling at Knocker. Although she could not understand Joe's words, the anger and frustration were clear. Knocker remained calm, though, trying to keep Joe at the dock. He was stalling Joe; they had to hurry!

When she saw Roselia's head above water, Michelle called to her. "Roselia, you need to call the crabs—have them follow your voice. I'll be too far away from them for the translation stone to work for many of them who will be closer to you, okay?"

"Got it, Michelle!" Roselia replied, then put her head back underwater to call the crabs. "This way everyone! We are making a slope so it is easier for you to get out of the pond. You must move as quickly as possible!"

Michelle lifted the tarp higher in the water, calling to the crabs on her side of the tarp. Roselia submerged and watched the crabs react to Michelle's instructions, and they all turned toward Roselia and headed her way.

"That's right!" Roselia encouraged them. "This way to escape!"

More crabs were heading her way, about half had already gotten out. "Keep coming this way!" Roselia called to them. "Go as fast as you can!"

Switching hands so her back was now facing the door opening, Michelle slowly raised the tarp edges over her back and pulled up, so her side was about three feet above Roselia's side and straight like a slide. "Slide down the tarp everyone, that's the way out!" She called out as she was lifting it higher. She hoped no humans were around to watch the spectacle!

As the crabs scurried down the slide, gravity helped them get through the door faster. Roselia waited at the other end, helping the crabs get through the slide and out of the way of the other crabs moving down into the water.

Michelle raised the tarp higher and higher until it was out of the water by about a foot and a half. Within a few minutes all the crabs had escaped into the river! Putting the tarp back underwater, Michelle stayed low and followed them to the door, folding up the tarp as she did; she didn't want to leave any evidence of their escape.

Roselia watched Michelle approaching the door and popped her head above the surface. "Michelle, thanks!" she said softly. "Let me help you fold up the tarp, and we'll let Knocker return it to the storage shed he borrowed it from."

Taking one side of the tarp, Roselia and Michelle folded it into a large square, which they placed on the seawall. "We have them all out now," Roselia exclaimed. "Our next step is to get them home. But first, we need to make sure Knocker can get out safely!"

Chapter Eleven

Covering Up the Escape

Voices could be heard from the direction of the dock; Roselia and Michelle turned, listening to shouting as Knocker and Joe were still arguing in the distance. Michelle could hear the voices getting louder and saw the guard heading toward the dock area. Roselia went under the water to talk to the horseshoe crabs waiting for her.

"Listen, everyone!" she called to them softly. "Stay here. I need you to form groups of about ten each and get ready to make a trip across the bay. The larger ones of the group will help the smaller ones. It is a long trek, so please rest and use this time to filter out the dirty water you had to breathe in the pond; you will need all your strength to get back home. We will be back shortly!"

Surfacing and turning to Michelle, she continued, "Michelle, we need to help Knocker get out of the situation he is in. I was remembering how hearing our mermaid siren made Joe leave earlier this evening, do you think it will work again? We need to get Knocker away without revealing the crabs are gone."

"Good idea, Roselia, it should work!" Michelle replied. "Call out to Knocker. Let him know the crabs are all out and you are ready to head back with them to get them home! Then you will need to leave as soon as possible!"

Michelle slipped through the door into the river and turned to close it. She was now in the river next to Roselia, but still in her human form.

"Listen, Roselia, I will stay here to make sure Knocker is safe." Michelle continued as she got closer. "Your mission is to get these crabs back to the ocean!"

Roselia nodded, knowing they needed to leave now, and called out loudly. "Knocker, our mission is accomplished! All the horseshoe crabs have been removed from the retention pond. The tarp is on the seawall. Michelle is staying to help you! I am leading the crabs away from the humans and back out to the ocean!"

Both Knocker and Joe stopped arguing and looked toward the source of the siren—past the dock and into the river. The guard stopped walking toward them, also turning to look at the river for the source of the siren. To humans like Joe, the message sounded like it was an emergency siren, possibly from a coast guard boat.

"Michelle," Roselia whispered, "Let's see what Knocker's response is, and then I'll leave with the crabs. You stay to be his back-up if needed."

"Agreed!" Michelle replied. "You make sure the crabs get back to the ocean, I'll be here for Knocker!"

Michelle and Roselia got closer to the dock to hear what Knocker would reply, and to hear what Joe's response would be. It was Knocker who reacted first.

"Joe, I think they are on to you!" Knocker said loudly. "Maybe you shouldn't have gone into the protected zone to capture the crabs."

"Who told you I did that!" Joe said angrily. "They were lying!"

"No, my friends saw you!" Knocker continued. "They must have reported you to the authorities. I am here to make sure you don't harm the crabs."

The guard was getting closer, walking faster as she was listening to their conversation. Soon she was next to Knocker and Joe.

"What do you know about this, young man?" she asked. "Why is this person on the company property?"

"A good friend of mine saw his boat capturing horseshoe crabs in the protected zone next to the beach," Knocker explained. "She called me and told me about it. I found the boat and made sure the crabs were not hurt. My friend is going to take them back home."

Roselia touched Michelle on the shoulder to get her attention. "Knocker has the situation in hand, you stay in the background, and help if needed. I'll be on my way with the crabs." Michelle nodded, and Roselia got ready for part three—get the crabs back home!

"Listen to me, my friends!" Roselia called softly. "I'm Roselia, and I'm here to take you back to the ocean. Each of you needs to stay with your group, help each other and stay together. Let me know if someone needs help—we need to do this together!"

"Thank you, Roselia. I'm Alicia. We have formed the groups like you said to do," said a crab close to Roselia. "We will follow you."

"We're ready!" said one crab.

"Thanks for coming for us, we will follow you back to our home!" said another.

"Okay, some of the larger of you stay to the outside, making sure we don't leave anyone behind," Roselia called. "Everyone, let's get started!"

Underwater, Roselia went to each group and got everyone lined up, each group about ten crabs across. "The stronger ones should be on the outside of your groups, so you can help the weaker ones along and they don't get lost!"

The loud rumble of a boat crossed the water very close to Roselia, and she went to the bottom of the river to avoid getting hit.

"The human must have left in a hurry!" Roselia called back. "Hopefully Knocker will be able to grab the tarp and he and Michelle can get away!"

Once the rumbling had passed, Roselia went to the front of the line and started the journey. "Let's get started!" she called back to them. "Stay together and follow me!" It would take several human hours to get these ancient warriors back to their home, and she hoped there were no more surprises!

Chapter Twelve

First Obstacles Encountered

Roselia looked ahead, trying to find the smoothest path while constantly checking back to make sure she wasn't swimming too fast. As a mermaid, items on the river bottom were not a worry, as she could swim over them. However, the crabs were walking, so anything that blocked their path could cause major issues.

Looking ahead, she saw what looked like a wall about a foot tall blocking their way. It stretched from one side of the river to the other as far as she could see.

"Alicia," she called back, "have you seen this before? How do you get around it?"

Alicia crawled over to Roselia and then inspected the barrier in front of them. She responded, "That looks like a large tree log I have seen before, although this type stretches from one shore to the other so we can't go around it. We will have to go over it!"

"How can we get the group across quickly?" Roselia asked. "You won't be able to crawl over it, it is too high. Possibly some of the largest crabs can swim over, but not everybody. Are there any other options?"

"The larger crabs can stand next to it and make a bridge," Alicia suggested. "I am one of the larger crabs here, so I can stay here and let the smaller crabs use me as a step to cross over the barrier, and you can watch as they cross over and help them get off the other side."

"That's a good plan!" Roselia agreed. "Please gather some of the larger horseshoe crabs to form a ramp up and over the wall on this side, and I will stay on the other side and help the crabs get over and down the other side. Let's get going!"

"We need several of the larger crabs. Please come now!" Alicia called out. "We need to make a pathway for the smaller crabs to get over this wall."

Twelve of the largest crabs came forward and started lining up in front of the wall.

"I will help the smaller crabs get started," said another. "And Roselia, you help them down the other side. Once we get most of them over, we will crawl up and over. Let's go!"

The large crabs formed two sets, the one closest to the wall was where eight of the larger crabs were located—four across with another set of four balancing on top of the first. The row farther away from the wall consisted of four crabs, creating steps for the smaller crabs to climb.

After the living stairway was completed, Roselia provided instructions. "Listen, my friends, these crabs have created steps so you can get over this object, as we can't go around it. I will be waiting on the other side to make sure you get down safely. Once over the ramp and down the other side, move ahead a little and then stop and wait for everyone else. We're all in this together!"

"Got it!" called a crab from the first group as he headed toward the ramp. "My group! Let's go two at a time, hurry now! Raphael, you take the back and help as needed—watch your sides—keep everyone moving at the same pace. Let's go!"

Watching the first group head up the ramp, Roselia hoped it would work. She saw the crabs climbing up, and she swam over to the other side to help them down. "Make sure you move out a bit so we can get everyone over. We have a way to go still!"

As two or three crabs came over at a time, Roselia would lift them and help them get down the other side. "Keep moving. We need you to reform your groups over here. Stay together and keep your buddies safe so we don't leave anyone behind! Group leaders, make sure all your group gets back together again!"

Alicia called out to her group, "All of my group, find Frederick and stay with him. I will look for him when I get over the wall!"

The other crabs started calling out also, making sure all the groups stayed together and reassembled.

Within a short time, they were able to get the crabs over the wall with Roselia helping the volunteers who formed the wall to get over also once the main group had passed.

"Great job, everyone!" Roselia called out. "Let me know when you have joined back with your groups, and we will continue our journey. I need to get you to the end of the river, so you can go back into the ocean and return home!"

"Alicia," exclaimed Frederick, "our group is over here!"

"Thanks, Frederick," Alicia replied. "I'm on my way!"

Roselia watched as the groups reformed, and then she swam to the front of the groups once they were all ready. "Let's continue!"

There were several docks that the procession needed to walk around, large poles blocking the way. The procession would stay on one side or the other and continue.

Roselia could see Alicia at the back of the procession and waved to her. "Is everything going okay back there?" She had noticed that Alicia seemed a little farther back than when they started.

"You may want to slow just a little!" Alicia replied. "It looks like some of the crabs are getting a little tired, and we need to make sure they have enough energy to make it the whole way!"

"Understood!" Roselia replied. "We will go a little slower. Keep me updated!"

"I will!" Alicia answered.

Roselia looked around, and they were about halfway back to the protected area that led to the ocean. To get there, they needed to pass through the channel used by human boats to go in between the ocean and river. The channel was a waterway that the humans had dredged up in the river as it reached the ocean, making it deep enough for large boats to pass through, and the protected area was on the other side of the channel. This was a scary place even for Roselia since many times the human boats had hooks or nets dragging behind them. Extra caution had to be used, even when mermaids passed through the channel.

To her troop of crabs, there would be two dangers—the drop off where it had been dredged, and the possibility of human boats attempting to trap them!

Chapter Thirteen

CROSSING THE CHANNEL

Roselia swam to the edge of the channel, and the light from the moon allowed her to see where the dredged area started. The slope down was sharp, and it was about five feet down to reach the lower level of the channel. Because it was night, she knew there wouldn't be as many human boats as there were during the day. However, the humans who were out at night were usually out to capture underwater creatures, just like the horseshoe crabs behind her. They would have to be careful!

Roselia swam back to the group and called out. "Listen carefully, my friends. We must cross quickly. Please keep your groups together so we can get through before one of the human boats comes by. Their large boats stir up the water and will make it difficult to cross. Remember, once we get across this channel, we are almost back to your home!"

Roselia looked back toward the river as she heard the low rumbling sound in the distance. She knew the sound meant that a human boat was heading out to the ocean and would be passing through the channel soon.

"Hurry! We must go now!" she called out. "Make sure you keep together with your group because, when the human boat goes by, the sands will be drawn up and start swirling, making it impossible to see."

Watching as the crabs scurried down the sharp slope, she hoped they would get across in time. It was very hard to predict how long it would take for a human boat to arrive and pass.

"Follow my voice!" she called out as the boat got closer. "I will be waiting on the other side, so you can hear which way to go!"

Swimming over to the upward slope, Roselia continued calling to the crabs, trying to be louder than the rumbling boat that was almost upon them.

"Keep moving! The down slope should be easy, then flat for several steps, and then head back up the slope." Roselia called out. Her calls were barely audible over the loud rumbling as the boat crossed above. She could see the sand being stirred up and whipping around in swirls as the propellers went by. "Keep following my voice, do not get turned around!"

Calling out continuously, she hoped that somewhere in the cloud of sand below her crabs had been able to keep heading toward her. "This way, everyone!"

Roselia waited on the other side, searching for her rescued horseshoe crabs. It was not much longer now; they were close to the protected area and to the deeper water. "Keep following my voice. I am waiting for you on the other side!"

"My group is almost there!" one crab called out. "Keep talking, as we can't see which way we should be heading!"

"Yes, I will!" Roselia responded. "Keep heading this way. This is the way to get back out of the channel! Once you start going up the slope, you are almost there!"

"Thanks!" was the reply. "We are on our way, doing our best!"

"Thank you—I'll keep talking. Just follow my voice!" Roselia said.

It took several minutes before the first group emerged from the swirling sands, and Roselia kept calling to them, letting them know which way to head. As the sand settled back down to the bottom and the water was clear again, she was relieved to see the rest of the groups of horseshoe crabs heading her way. She could hear another rumbling, which meant another human boat was approaching, and she needed to get them out before the next one passed overhead.

"Thank you, everyone, you are almost through the channel!" she called out. "You can make it! Keep moving until you are out of the channel, and make sure all your group stays together!"

Roselia could hear the crabs talking among themselves, checking to make sure they had all their group with them. "Everyone, gather near me on this side so we can make sure all made it through!"

"Roselia," Alicia called to her. "We will need to rest for a minute. The steep slope getting out of the channel was tiring. Please give us a few minutes before heading on!"

"Yes, I agree, please take a rest for a few minutes!" Roselia replied. "I am so glad you all have made it this far. There is not much farther to go, and no obstacles that I remember. There are some patches of tall seagrasses, but that should not be too much of a problem."

"Thank you, Roselia, for all your help!" called out Frederick. "We will be ready to start again in a few minutes."

"I'm going to swim ahead to see if there is anything we need to worry about. I will be back shortly!" Roselia called as she headed toward the protected area.

Okay," Frederick replied. "We will rest while you check our path to the ocean. Thanks!"

For Roselia, the protected area was only a few tail strokes away, and she was soon back where she had been several hours ago watching the horseshoe crabs first emerging from the depths. So much had happened in such a short period of time, and she was glad that Knocker and Michelle were able to assist in freeing the crabs. They were almost home!

A shadow over her head drew her attention to the surface, and as she looked up through the water, she saw a human boat, either the same one as before or a similar one, slowly coming back into the protected zone.

No! This can't happen again!

Chapter Fourteen

Back to Where It Began

Roselia headed to the surface because she had to see what was going on in the shallows where she was leading the crabs. She needed to make sure they would be safe!

As she surfaced, she saw that it was Joe. He was back, and he was ready to jump into the water to capture more crabs!

Looking in the direction of the beach, she saw the shadow of a human standing on the beach also—she would need to turn the crabs around and get them away from the protected area, even if it meant crossing the dangerous channel again!

Roselia submerged under the water—she needed a few moments to figure out what her next steps would be. A human boat and someone standing on the beach: they blocked the way back to the ocean. What chance did the crabs have?

As she was thinking about the change needed in her plans, she heard voices—the human on the boat and the person on the beach were shouting at each other. She raised her head above the water to see if she could get some idea of what was going on—even if she could not understand, she could tell the emotions that were going back and forth, were they working together or against each other? Working against each other might be to her advantage.

As she surfaced, she was surprised that she could understand one of the voices, it was Knocker! Wading out into the shallows where Joe had stopped his boat, Knocker got close enough for his translation stone to work.

"Joe," Knocker called out. "You are not to be here. My friends are watching you!"

Joe yelled back angrily. Roselia could not understand what he was saying, but he was very angry at Knocker. She moved closer but stayed out of Joe's sight; she needed to get within ten feet of Knocker's translation stone. She needed to know what was happening!

Being very close now to Knocker and hiding just behind Joe's boat, she could understand Joe as he screamed at Knocker.

"I can be wherever I want to be, and there's nothing you can do about it, got that?" Joe yelled menacingly.

"I have given you fair warning, and my friends are not as accepting as I am!" Knocker said, continuing to wade into the shallow water so he could keep within ten feet of Joe. The boat was drifting slowly into deeper water. "Is poaching these crabs worth the loss of your boat? If you do not leave now, you will lose your boat!"

"What are you talking about? You are crazy. There ain't nothing that can hurt this boat. I've had it for

years!" Joe replied in a nasty tone. "You might want to leave now, though, before something bad happens to you!"

"My friends, this poacher of sea creatures has decided to forfeit his boat." Knocker called loudly. "I need your help!"

Roselia knew that Knocker was depending on her and her pod to get rid of this danger, so she issued a call under the water. "I need help! Anyone in the area, please come now!" Joe would not be able to hear it because she called under the water—and under water, the call for help traveled quickly.

She listened anxiously for a response, and she did not have to wait long. Yes, there were other members of the pod in the area, and they had heard her call.

She heard a reply. "I'm on my way!"

"Roselia, we will be there shortly!" came another response soon after.

"Well, boy, it looks like your friends have abandoned you!" Joe said angrily after waiting for a response from land and hearing no response to Knocker's call for help.

"I think not," Knocker said calmly; then he pointed out to sea.

"What are you pointing at? I don't see any boats out there!" Joe called out as he glanced quickly toward the open water and back at Knocker. "You are bluffing!"

As Knocker continued pointing, Joe looked again, trying to find what Knocker was pointing at. He searched for lights on a boat, then started scanning the surface of the water. His eyes widened as he saw it—the moonlight revealed several large wakes in the water heading their way, indicating that large creatures were swimming just underneath the water.

"What are you pointing at?" Joe yelled, concern creeping into his voice as he tried to figure out what the wakes meant. "I don't see any boats—where are your friends?"

"This is your last chance!" Knocker said. He was waist-deep in the water now, staying within the translation stone's range. "Leave this area and never return, or your boat will be taken to the depths!"

Joe's boat had drifted out to where the water was about four feet deep. Roselia was close enough now so she could reach out and touch Joe's boat.

Pushing on one side of the boat, she started rocking it back and forth slowly.

"Roselia," called Alleana as she swam up to help, "I'm here! What do you need?"

"Hi, Alleana, thank you for coming!" She replied gratefully. "We need to make this human and its boat leave the protected area. Knocker is on the surface telling him that he can no longer enter these waters safely. We need to let him know there is danger here for him!"

Roselia and Alleana started pushing on one side of the boat, moving it around and making banging noises on the hull by striking it with their hands.

"Thank you, Cristiana for your help!" Roselia called out as another mermaid joined the group. "Please stay here with Alleana; I'm going to the surface for a moment listen to Knocker's conversation, so we can determine how to respond!" Surfacing close to the boat on the opposite side so Joe could not see her, Roselia made sure she would be close enough to have Knocker's translation stone relay Joe's side of the conversation.

"This boat is here to steal more creatures from this protected area, and we can't allow this!" Knocker said.

"What is happening?" Joe cried out in panic. "What is attacking my boat? How are you doing this?"

"Those are my friends!" Knocker replied confidently. "I never said my friends were human!"

Chapter Fifteen

Mermaids to the Rescue

"What do you mean?" Joe asked as he held tightly onto the side of his boat. "What are you doing to my boat?"

Roselia swam behind the boat and slapped her tail on the water, making a large splash and the resulting waves hit the boat. She needed to make as much noise as possible to make it sound like there were many sea creatures in the water!

"The sea creatures are exacting their revenge on you. They have watched you harm and kill their friends, and yesterday, they reported to me you were stealing crabs from their protected area, and they are angry! Your only choice, if you want to save your boat, is to leave this area and never return to the waters here. Otherwise, your boat will not survive. What is your answer?" Knocker's voice was demanding, showing that he was not going to put up with Joe's arrogance anymore.

Roselia joined Alleana and Christiana near the bottom of the boat. "We need to make noise and make the human think his boat is in danger!" she said. "Knocker is telling him he must leave now and never come back. Let's make sure he gets the message!"

Getting under the boat, Roselia started banging on the bottom while Alleana and Christiana kept it rocking and spinning.

"Great work!" Roselia said, "Let me see what they are saying now! Keep rocking the boat!"

Surfacing once again, she saw Joe's boat was drifting into the shallows now, and Joe was hanging off one side. Knocker was only a few feet away from him, still waist-deep in the water.

"Tell them to leave me alone!" he begged, clinging to the side rail. "I'll leave now and not come back!"

"Is that a promise?" Knocker asked. "If so, I will let them know. I am sure that they will find you if you break your promise!"

"Yes, I promise," Joe said dejectedly. "I will never come into the protected area again. Just tell them to let me go!"

"My friends, this human is leaving now and has promised not to return," Knocker called out into the darkness of the night.

Turning to Joe, he continued. "Your boat has been marked. Should you ever break your promise, the sea creatures will claim your boat as punishment. Now leave!"

Roselia submerged and quickly swam over to the mermaids. "Okay, he has promised to leave and never come back!" she said quickly. "We need to stop and get out of his way so we don't get hit by the boat."

Alleana and Christiana nodded and swam into deeper water, getting away from the shore and the vicinity of Joe's boat.

"Why don't we go check on the horseshoe crabs?" Roselia said to her fellow mermaids. "I left them just on this side of the channel. They needed to take a short rest before heading this way and having to deal with the long seagrass. Let the boat leave and then follow me!"

The mermaids could hear the rumble as the boat was starting its engines and watched as it quickly headed toward the channel. "Okay, he's gone. Let me show you the crabs so you can check on them, and then I'll come back and check with Knocker."

Roselia swam quickly to where she had left the horseshoe crabs, and they were gathered waiting for her return.

"Alicia," Roselia called. "I have brought some mermaid friends who can lead you back to the area where you were captured. This is Alleana and Christiana; they will help you get ready for the final portion of your journey. I will return shortly, and we will all go together to the safe area."

"Alleana, I'll be back as soon as I talk with Knocker," Roselia said.

"Yes, Roselia, I agree," Alleana replied. "Make sure everything is good with Knocker and then return, and we will finish the journey."

Turning quickly, Roselia swam back to the shallow area where she had last seen Knocker.

Surfacing, she looked around to make sure Joe was gone and then called out. "Knocker, are you still here?"

"Yes, Roselia," Knocker replied softly. "Over here!"

Wading out until he was waist-deep in the water, Knocker waited for Roselia to swim closer.

"Great job, Roselia!" Knocker said as she surfaced next to him. "You scared Joe so bad that he has promised never to return to this protected area. At least that is one less human to have to worry about!"

"Thanks!" she replied. "Thank you for getting him to leave, Knocker; and I am glad that we don't have to worry about him again."

"Were you able to get the crabs here? Do you need any more help?" Knocker asked.

"Alleana and Christiana came to help me with the boat, and they are with the crabs now," Roselia replied. "We have only to get through the grasses, and they will be able to go back into the deep water again. I'll need to go help them, but I wanted to thank you first for coming to help me rescue them!"

"You are welcome. I am always glad to help my friends!" Knocker said, smiling at Roselia. "You did the right thing. I was able to get Michelle home so no need to worry about her. One quick thing: I was able to talk to the guard. I told her that we had seen the crabs taken from the protected area, and that was why we were freeing them."

"What did she say?" asked Roselia, "Can we count on her not to let it happen again?"

"Well, since there were no crabs in the pond, she couldn't charge Joe with poaching them from the protected area," Knocker replied. "But she did say that she would carefully watch, and if anyone tries to sneak in crabs at night again, she will get law enforcement involved. She also said that she would be glad to assist in the future if I or my friends saw any other illegal activities going on. We have a new friend to help our sea creature friends! Michelle has her contact information, so please get in touch with Michelle if you need assistance in the future."

"That is great news!" Roselia replied, so glad that there was a human willing to help protect her friends. "And between you, Michelle, and our new friend, we have saved our horseshoe crab friends! Thank you!"

"Be safe, my friend!" Knocker said, bowing his head with respect. "And always remember I am available to help whenever needed. Farewell for now!"

Chapter Sixteen

Returning Home

Roselia waved goodbye as she watched Knocker transform back into a dragon and take off into the night. As soon as he was out of sight, she headed back to where the crabs were waiting. She still had to complete her mission—to get these crabs safely back to their home!

In just a few moments, Roselia reached where Alleana and Christiana were talking with the many horseshoe crabs who had been rescued.

"Roselia," Alleana called as Roselia swam up, "Alicia has been telling me of your brave actions in rescuing them and getting them this far. Well done!"

"Thank you, Alleana," Roselia responded. "We were lucky to have Knocker and Michelle to help, and the crabs were also great! And thank you and Christiana for answering my call! Between all of us, acting together as a team, we were successful in our rescue. We only have a small distance now to get this group back home!"

"I agree!" Alleana said. "Let's get these crabs through the tall grasses and back to the protected area, then they can go back home! What is your plan?"

"Well, much of the long grass areas we can walk around. However, there are a few rows that are blocking the way," Roselia replied. "If you are able to stay for a short time, maybe you, Christiana, and I can use our tails to hold the long grasses to the sides so the crabs can travel through them to the protected area and the ocean beyond."

Christiana, who was next to Alleana, agreed. "Roselia, I think that is a great idea! Alleana and I can each take a side, and you can lead them down the middle, making sure there is a clear path for them to get by. We can swim together to make them a path!"

"Sounds great," Alleana responded. "Let's get started!"

"Gather 'round, my friends!" Roselia called to the crabs. "We only have one area left to get through as a group. The tall grasses ahead might be difficult for you to get through after your ordeal today. We will walk around the grass when we are able, and if needed, the mermaids will hold the long grasses down so you can crawl over them. Once we get set up, you can crawl between the mermaids and on top of the folded grass."

Alicia responded. "That sounds like it will work. Let's get everyone lined up. We have been able to rest and are ready to get home!"

The mermaids watched as the horseshoe crabs moved around, talking to each other, and the leaders checking to make sure all their group was together.

Once they were lined up and ready, Frederick called out, "Roselia, we are ready! Let's go!"

Roselia took the lead, weaving with the crabs back and forth across the sandy area, avoiding the clumps of seagrass. When they encountered a large section of grass too large to go around, Alleana and Christiana used their tails to hold down on the grass forming a path for the crabs to crawl over. Roselia would help the crabs crawl over and get through the grassy area. There were only a few of these, and everyone worked together to get through them.

Seeing the protected area again, Roselia turned around and called back to her horseshoe crabs assembled behind. "We are there!" she called back to them.

"Yes, we made it!" Alicia called out. "We made it, everyone!"

Happy cries were heard from the crabs, so glad to have made it back to where they had been taken.

"Let's go back to the deep!" one called.

"We have been rescued. Thank you so much!" said another.

Roselia watched as the crabs went from the shallows of the protected area back to the deeper zones, back to where they were safe. They moved faster, bumping into each other; they were excited to reach the entrance to the deeper water. Many called out "Thank you!" as they disappeared into the darkness of the deep.

"Roselia, you did it!" Alleana said once all the crabs had passed by and returned to their homes. "I am so proud of how you took over the situation and rescued these noble creatures. Your dedication to our mission to protect all sea creatures is admirable, and because of you, these creatures were able to return home. Thank you!"

"Thanks, Alleana, I could not leave when I saw the danger facing the crabs and knew that rescuing them was the right thing to do! I know your rule is not to be seen, and I made sure that I was not seen by any humans—any human but Michelle of course!" Roselia replied.

"You did the right thing, Roselia," Alleana responded warmly, "as these horseshoe crabs would have suffered if you had not acted on their behalf. Your plan was great, and including Knocker and Michelle worked very well. I want to thank you for completing your mission and getting these ancient warriors back to their home.

"Now, you have had a very exciting evening!" Alleana remarked. "Let's all head home together, and you can tell me all about your adventure!"

"Yes, Alleana!" Roselia agreed. "It was a very exciting evening, and I'm glad that we had a happy ending. I would love to tell you all about it!"

As they swam back to the mermaid pod caves, Roselia thought about her adventure today and was glad that she had taken action to protect the crabs. It was good to know that, at least for tonight, the protected area was still a safe place for the horseshoe crabs. She would remain vigilant in the days to come to make sure they remained safe from humans while in the protected area.

THE END—*until Roselia's next adventure!*

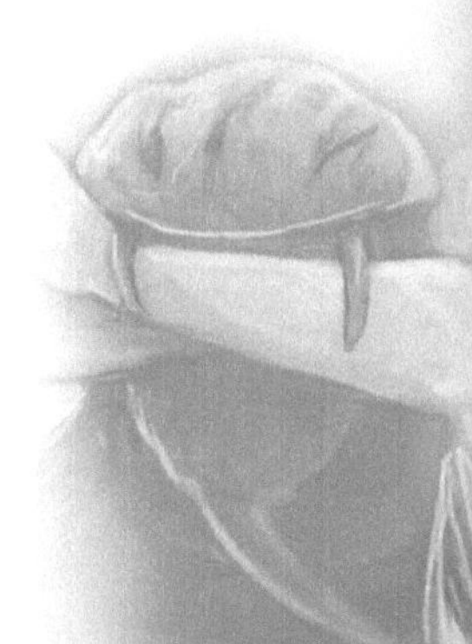

Note From Author

Although this is a fantasy adventure, the danger to horseshoe crabs is real. The demand for horseshoe crab blood has grown enormously for use in medical laboratories. It endangers both the crabs and the many species that depend on them to survive, including the Rufa Red Knot, which depend on the eggs laid by these sea creatures in order to make their migration from South America to the Arctic.

As the demand increases, there are fewer and fewer horseshoe crabs to be found. Although the laboratories claim that they do no harm and let the crabs go after they draw out 30 percent of the blood, reports show that up to 30 percent of the crabs die after this procedure, and many more appear lethargic with a decreased ability to survive. While a synthetic option has been created as an acceptable substitute for horseshoe crab blood, it appears to be easier just to continue capturing and draining these creatures, with little regard to the effects of such bleeding on the crabs and on the creatures that depend on them and their eggs to survive.

They have survived as a species for hundreds of millions of years, earning the name of "ancient warriors" because they have survived even longer than the dinosaurs. While they are considered valuable for their blood and are also caught to use as bait, their numbers are declining greatly, and the animals that depend on them to survive, like the Rufa Red Knot, are also declining at a drastic rate. Only a realistic survival plan, and enforcement of that plan, will preserve and protect these wonderful creatures and ensure they will survive to continue their legacy. We cannot let these beautiful creatures, these ancient warriors, disappear into the past!

For more information on Horseshoe Crabs, check out the following:

Horseshoe crab blood saves lives. Can we protect these animals from ourselves? (nationalgeographic.com) by Dina Maron

Horseshoe Crab | Defenders of Wildlife

11 Facts About Horseshoe Crabs That Will Blow Your Mind - Ocean Conservancy

Horseshoe Crab | National Wildlife Federation (nwf.org)

Book Club Questions

1. Why was Roselia watching the horseshoe crabs?

2. How does she contact Knocker the dragon?

3. Why do they need to give the horseshoe crabs water while they are in the boat?

4. What was the original purpose of putting a tarp in the retention pond?

5. Why did they change their plans regarding the use of the tarp?

6. To what group/species are horseshoe crabs most closely related?

7. Why are medical laboratories requiring so many horseshoe crabs? Are there any alternatives?

8. Why is the decrease in the number of horseshoe crabs also affecting other creatures, for example, the Rufa Red Knot?

9. How did Roselia and Knocker get Joe to leave the protected area when he returned to capture more crabs?

10. Something to think about—is there a solution to the ever-growing demand for horseshoe crabs that is causing their rapid decline? What if the increasing demand ultimately results in no more horseshoe crabs to generate the blood needed by the labs? What then? What can we do to protect these ancient warriors now from becoming just another creature who became extinct because of human indifference and short-sightedness?

About The Author

J.B. moved to Florida in her early teens and has lived there ever since, enjoying the mild weather and abundance of wildlife. She even spent several seasons raising orphan squirrels. She graduated from the University of Central Florida and has spent her working career in the legal profession. Her novels are inspired by her family and nature, as well as her need to escape from the real world once in a while.

www.facebook.com/J.B.Moonstar

Instagram@J.B.Moonstar

Twitter@jb_moonstar

Jbmoonstar.author@gmail.com

Website – www.jbmoonstar.com

Discover More by JB Moonstar

Chronicles of Ituria

Russ and The Hidden Voice

Taylor and the Red Wolf Rescue

Jenna and the Legend of the White Wolf

Jenna and the Eyes of Fire

Jan and the Secret Cave

Jan and the Search for Lilya

Taylor and the Final Nine

Michelle and the Missing Manatee

Jenna and the Broken Promise

Sara and the Secret Mission

& More Adventures to Come!

The Mermaids of Crystal Cay

Kimmi and the Sea Dragon

Roselia and the Ancient Warriors

& More Adventures to Come!

Coloring Book from

Artist Jenn Kotick

Mermaids

Discover more at
4HorsemenPublications.com

10% off using HORSEMEN10